READ HIB

Traps and Snai

S0-AJO-809

DATE

A Note to Parents

DK READERS is a compelling program for beginning readers, designed in conjunction with leading literacy experts, including Dr. Linda Gambrell, Professor of Education at Clemson University. Dr. Gambrell has served as President of the International Reading Association, National Reading Conference, and the College Reading Association.

Beautiful illustrations and superb full-color photographs combine with engaging, easy-to-read stories to offer a fresh approach to each subject in the series. Each DK READER is guaranteed to capture a child's interest while developing his or her reading skills, general knowledge, and love of reading.

The five levels of DK READERS are aimed at different reading abilities, enabling you to choose the books that are exactly right for your child:

Pre-level 1: Learning to read
Level 1: Beginning to read
Level 2: Beginning to read alone
Level 3: Reading alone
Level 4: Proficient readers

The "normal" age at which a child begins to read can be anywhere from three to eight years old. Adult participation through the lower levels is very helpful for providing encouragement, discussing storylines, and sounding out unfamiliar words.

No matter which level you select, you can be sure that you are helping your child learn to read, then read to learn!

LONDON, NEW YORK, MUNICH,
MELBOURNE, AND DELHI

For Dorling Kindersley
Project Editor Heather Scott
Designer Hanna Ländin
Managing Editor Catherine Saunders
Art Director Lisa Lanzarini
Publishing Manager Simon Beecroft
Category Publisher Alex Allan
Production Editor Clare McLean
Production Controller Poppy Newdick

For Lucasfilm
Executive Editor Jonathan W. Rinzler
Art Director Troy Alders
Keeper of the Indycron Leland Chee
Director of Publishing Carol Roeder

Reading Consultant
Linda B. Gambrell, Ph.D

First published in the United States by
DK Publishing, 375 Hudson Street,
New York, New York 10014

09 10 11 12 10 9 8 7 6 5 4 3 2 1
DD546—07/09

DK books are available at special discounts when purchased in bulk
for sales promotions, premiums, fund-raising, or educational use.
For details, contact:
DK Publishing Special Markets
375 Hudson Street
New York, New York 10014
SpecialSales@dk.com

A catalog record for this book is available
from the Library of Congress.

ISBN: 978-0-7566-5527-3 (Paperback)
ISBN: 978-0-7566-5526-6 (Hardcover)

Color reproduction by MDP, UK
Printed and bound in the U.S.A. by Lake Book Manufacturing, Inc.

Discover more at
www.dk.com
www.starwars.com

DK READERS

BEGINNING
TO READ ALONE
2

Traps and Snares

Written by Clare Hibbert

Join Indiana Jones on his travels in search of treasure. Indy looks for many precious objects around the world.

The searches are never easy. Indy often sets off traps. Oh no! This time a giant ball of rock is rolling after him!

In Peru, Indy is on the trail of a golden idol. He soon finds out what happened to his friend, Doctor Forrestal. He crossed a beam of sunlight, which set off spring-loaded spears. Quick and deadly! Only Forrestal's skeleton remains.

Sinister statue
This statue is located near the temple entrance to scare people away.

Indy soon finds out that he has more to fear than spears. Many of the stone tiles on the floor are traps, too. If Indy steps on one, poison-tipped arrows shoot at him from the walls.

Indy now understands that the whole temple is booby-trapped. If he removes the idol, he knows something terrible will happen.

Indy wants to trick the
temple. He has a little
sack of sand. His plan is
to switch the idol for the

Golden idol

sack, which weighs
about the same. At least,
he hopes it weighs the same.
Oh no! The sand is too heavy!

The stone altar that holds the icon lowers into its base. Indy has set off a chain reaction that causes the ancient temple to seal itself. Indy barely escapes—but then he is chased by a tribe of angry Hovitos.

Oh no! Indy falls off the edge of
a cliff while on top of a tank. He
jumps off the tank just in time
and grabs a tree root.

Indy is looking for the Holy Grail. It is hidden in an ancient temple. When the Grail is carried over a sacred mark on the ground, an earthquake starts! Indy falls into a crack in the rocks. The Grail is almost within Indy's grasp—but he might fall if he tries to reach it!

Indy's hunt for a sacred stone takes him to Pankot Palace. With his friend, Short Round, he explores a secret passage. Where does it lead? Someone does not want them to know. The two are trapped in a mysterious room!

Pankot Palace

Poor Short Round leans against a stone set into the wall. Uh oh! Now the ceiling starts coming down—with spikes!

Hidden temple

The traps keep outsiders from a temple. Here, worshippers sacrifice people to their goddess, Kali.

Indy, Willie, and Short Round free
the children forced to work in the
terrible mines of Pankot Palace.

Now they are stuck in a runaway
mine car. Indy jumps out and
stops the mine car with his feet.

Then a huge water tank is tipped
over. Water gushes through the
tunnels. The three find a way out
just in time. A moment later, the
flood bursts
out of the
tunnel—and
almost knocks
them off
the cliff.

Imagine being trapped on a rickety old rope bridge, surrounded by enemies. Hungry crocodiles wait below. What would you do?

Indy cuts through the rope—and clings on for dear life.

Rope bridge

The broken bridge swings against
the cliff. Indy struggles with Mola
Ram. The priest wants the sacred
stones in Indy's satchel. Mola
Ram loses his grip and falls into
the river. The crocodiles gobble
him up.

For Indy, even a plane can be
a trap. After he escapes
the Hovitos tribe, he finds a
snake in his seat! Indy is afraid of
snakes. He and Marion need to
escape from Egypt in a plane. But
first Indy
must face
an angry
mechanic.

On another adventure, Indy, Willie, and Short Round are on a plane. But the pilots empty the fuel, take the only parachutes, and jump out. Indy is trapped onboard with a cargo of squawking chickens!

Life-saving raft
Indy jumps from the plane with an inflatable raft. They go whooshing over snowy slopes and waterfalls!

Indy is as brave as they come, but he isn't crazy about snakes. As a boy he had no fear. But that all changes the day he falls into a box full of the slithering reptiles! He is completely covered with snakes!

Creepy cobra
Poor Indy. He's always coming face to face with sinister snakes. This cobra is a bit too close for comfort.

In Egypt, Indy sneaks into a place called the Well of Souls. The floor is a sea of snakes. His flaming torch keeps the scary serpents away for a little while. But when the flame goes out, the snakes start to close in.

Indy meets more than his fair share of creepy crawlies and scary animals.

In Venice, Indy and Elsa are looking for a knight's tomb. They step along flooded tunnels that are plagued with rats.

The rainforest has the deadliest
bugs. Indy and his guide, Satipo,
are covered with tarantulas. And
Indy's enemy, Colonel Dovchenko,
is attacked by red ants.

Red ant

Jagged jaws

Indy and his father, Henry, are on a beach. Suddenly, they are fired on by a German plane. Surely there is no escape this time! But Henry has an idea. He flaps his umbrella at the seagulls. The frightened flock flies into the air and makes the plane crash.

When Indy was a boy scout, he
uncovered a plot to steal the
Cross of Coronado. But he grabs
the cross and escapes onto a
circus train. The thieves chase
him, but Indy gets away again.

Indiana Jones teams up with his son, Mutt, on a quest to find Akator, the Lost City of Gold.

Indy wants to return a strange Crystal Skull to the ancient temple. But many traps and snares block his path. In a round tower, the adventurers must dash down the steps before they disappear into the wall. If Indy isn't fast enough, he will fall onto spikes below.

Hordes of Ugha warriors ambush Indy and his friends in a secret tunnel. They run after Indy, Professor Oxley, and Mutt.

Don't trip, Mutt!

Oxley holds the Crystal Skull that he is taking back to Akator. The warriors see it and give up the chase.

It's not the first time Indy's been ambushed. After finding the golden idol, he thinks he's safe once he exits the temple.

Not so! Suddenly he is face-to-face with a tribe of Hovitos. They

are armed with poison arrows. Run, Indy!

Being double-crossed by a friend
is one of the worst traps of all.
Mac betrays Indy at a secret
army base.

Mac sides with the Russians, so
Indy is forced to find a mysterious
box for Colonel Spalko.

Later, Mac convinces Indy that he is a double agent. It's a trick! Mac is leaving a trail so the Russians can follow Indy.

Power seeker
Spalko will stop at nothing to gain power. But this power destroys her and Mac in the end.

Fascinating Facts

• The monkey that becomes Marion's pet in Cairo is a false friend. It is really a spy, keeping tabs on Indy for a shadowy assassin.

• Indy guesses that there are secret tunnels beneath Pankot Palace. He notices a breeze blowing the flowers in Willie's room.

• To reach the Grail, Indy must make a leap of faith. What looks like a gaping chasm is really spanned by an invisible bridge.

• The glittering grails around the true Grail are traps. When Walter Donovan chooses a fake, it doesn't give him long life—it kills him.

• Indy and Mutt face an array of traps and snares while they search for a grave. There are venomous scorpions, and a "dead end" that turns out to be a tilting stone.